IGGY
IGUANODON

Playtime & Mealtime

Time to Read

Time to Read® is an early reader program designed to guide children to literacy success regardless of age or grade level. The program's three levels correspond to stages of reading readiness, making book selection straightforward, and assuring that when it's time for a child to read, the right book is waiting.

— Level —
1

Beginning to Read
- Large, simple type
- Basic vocabulary
- Word repetition
- Strong illustration support

— Level —
2

Reading with Help
- Short sentences
- Engaging stories
- Simple dialogue
- Illustration support

— Level —
3

Reading Independently
- Longer sentences
- Harder words
- Short paragraphs
- Increased story complexity

For Greta—MM

For Lynda & Paul, the best aunt & uncle
a small dinosaur could ever have!—JF

Library of Congress Cataloging-in-Publication data
is on file with the publisher.
Text copyright © 2020 Maryann Macdonald
Illustrations copyright © 2020 Albert Whitman & Company
Illustrations by Jo Fernihough
First published in the United States of America in 2020
by Albert Whitman & Company
ISBN 978-0-8075-3642-1 (hardcover)
ISBN 978-0-8075-3645-2 (ebook)

TIME TO READ® is a registered trademark of Albert Whitman & Company.

Printed in China

10 9 8 7 6 5 4 3 2 1 HH 24 23 22 21 20

Design by Heather Barber

For more information about Albert Whitman & Company,
visit our website at www.albertwhitman.com

IGGY
IGUANODON

Playtime & Mealtime

Maryann Macdonald

illustrated by
Jo Fernihough

Albert Whitman & Company
Chicago, Illinois

Playtime

Iggy Iguanodon's brother, Stoog, is going to the river with his friend Dreet. "Dreet's going to teach me to swim," Stoog brags. "We might go fishing too!"

"Can I come?" asks Iggy.
"No way," says Stoog.
"Please!" begs Iggy.

"Sorry," says Stoog.
"I don't think Dreet likes
tagalongs."

"Never mind," says Mama.
"Mrs. Macrosaur is coming
over today.
She is bringing her little
daughter, Murka.
You can play with her."

"That won't be any fun,"
says Iggy.
"Don't be silly," says Mama.
"Murka is a very nice little
triceratops.
I know you two will have
a nice time together."

No, we won't, thinks Iggy.
What if Murka wants to
play some dumb game like
paleo princess?

And she'll probably cry
if I won't be the prince.

But Murka is not the
princess type.

"What do you want
to play?" asks Iggy.

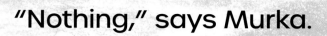
"Nothing," says Murka.

"How about hopscotch?"
asks Iggy.

But Murka is hopeless
at hopscotch.

"Want to do somersaults?"
says Iggy.

But Murka gets stuck in somersaults, the same as all triceratops.

"Let's try leapfrog!" says Iggy.

But Murka is dangerous at leapfrog because of her horn.

Iggy thinks and thinks.
"What about ring toss?"

Murka is great at ring toss,
like all triceratops!
So is Iggy.
They play all afternoon.

"Did you learn how to swim?"
Iggy asks Stoog later.
"Some dinosaurs are not
meant to swim," says Stoog.

"Did you catch any fish?"
"They were not biting,"
says Stoog. "What did
you do?"

"I made a new friend,"
says Iggy.
"We had a blast!
I'm going to play with her
tomorrow."

"Can I come?" asks Stoog. "Please?"

"I'll ask Murka," says Iggy.

"I don't know
if she likes tagalongs."

Mealtime

Iggy Iguanodon is not
eating his dinner.
It smells funny.
It looks yucky.
"I hate ferns," Iggy says.

"How do you know?"
asks Mama.
"You've never tasted them."

"A growing dinosaur needs his greens," says Papa.
"Eat up, my boy."
"I'm not hungry," says Iggy.

So Mama takes the
ferns away.
Then she puts out
a big pile of flowers.

They smell sweet.
They look delicious.
"Mmmmmmm," says Iggy.
"I'm hungry now."

"Too bad," says Papa.
"Anyone who won't eat
their greens can't have
any flowers."

"Excuse me," says Iggy.
He gets up and walks away.
He goes to his secret place
to be sad.

But Grandpa Dinosaur
finds him.
"Don't cry," he says.

"There will be more
flowers tomorrow."
"Tomorrow?"
says Iggy.
He can't wait *that* long.

"In my day," says Grandpa, "all we ate were ferns and leaves. We never had any flowers. So I don't really like them. I saved mine for you."

Iggy looks at the flowers
Grandpa gives him.
Then he looks at Grandpa.
"How do you know you don't
like them?" he asks.
"You've never tasted them."

"All right," says Grandpa. "I'll try a flower if you'll try a fern."

"You first," says Iggy.
So Grandpa takes one
pink flower and puts it
into his mouth.
He chews it.
He swallows it.
"Not bad," he says.

Iggy looks for a fern.
He picks the smallest
one he can find.

He puts it into his mouth.
He chews it.
Then he spits it out.
"Ugh! Tastes terrible,"
he says.

"At least you tried it,"
says Grandpa.
"Yes, I tried playing with Murka.
And I tried eating ferns!"
"Two new things,"
says Grandpa.

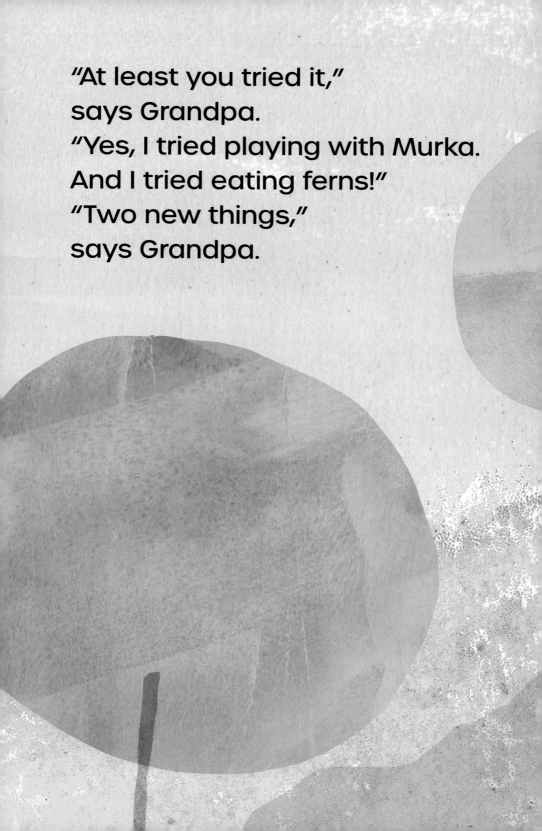

"One good, one not so good,"
says Iggy.
Then they take turns
eating all the rest
of the sweet pink flowers,
one by one.